THE TOPSY-TURVY TEACHER

OTHER JUPITER JANE ADVENTURES:

The Apple Pie Alien
The Boggy Bay Marathon
Spots in Space

ORCHARD BOOKS
96 Leonard Street, London EC2A 4RH
ORCHARD BOOKS AUSTRALIA
14 Mars Road, Lane Cove, NSW 2066
ISBN 1 85213 517 4

First published in Great Britain 1988
First paperback publication 1994
Text copyright © Sheila Lavelle 1988
Illustrations copyright © Sue Heap 1994

Printed and bound in Great Britain

A CIP catalogue record for this book is available from the British Library.

The Topsy-Turvy
TEACHER

Sheila Lavelle

Illustrated by Sue Heap

ORCHARD BOOKS

Chapter One

Katy Stuart, looking out of the backseat window, knew that something awful had happened as soon as the car turned into the drive. Securely locked before they left, the garage doors were now swinging open in the wind, and several of the family's belongings lay scattered about on the ground.

"Good grief!" said Katy's dad, leaping out of the car and running towards the garage. "We've been burgled!"

Katy's mum heaved herself out of the front passenger seat and slammed the car door hard. "You can't have locked up properly!" she shouted after her husband accusingly. "They'd better not have pinched my bits of silver, or you'll be in trouble." She unlocked the front door and marched into the house.

Katy, hunched miserably in the corner, glanced sideways at the astonished face of her companion.

"What does he mean, burgled?" Jane demanded, wide-eyed. "Surely Earth people don't still go round stealing each other's things?" She tossed her blonde pigtails disgustedly. "I knew Earth was a horrible planet, but I didn't know it was this horrible."

"We'd better go in and see," said Katy

wearily. "They might have taken that box of stuff you brought with you from Jupiter."

Jane scrambled hastily out of the car. "My computer!" she wailed, dashing into the house and up the stairs, her orange webbed feet skidding on the carpet.

Katy sighed as she followed her in. What a thing to happen. They'd only been away for a week's holiday. It was bad enough having an alien from space staying with them, spoiling their peaceful life, spying on everything they did, and writing reports all the time to send back to Jupiter, without being burgled as well. Now Jupiter Jane was bound to make a bad report to the Inter-planetary Relations Board, just when they were beginning to get on a bit better. Life could be very unfair sometimes, Katy thought.

Mr Stuart made a rapid tour of the rooms and came into the hall. He blinked behind his thick glasses like a short-sighted owl.

"It's not too bad," he told Katy with relief. "It was probably just a gang of kids. They didn't get into the house at all, thanks to those new locks we had fitted. But there's quite of lot of stuff missing from the garage. Tools and things. And they took your bike, I'm afraid."

Katy put her arms round him. "That's all right, Dad," she said. "I don't mind." It was the truth. She hadn't wanted a bike in the first place. Cycling was far too energetic a pastime for Katy, whose favourite occupation was dozing in the sun with a book in her lap. Being bone idle, her mum called it.

Jane pushed rudely past on her way out to the garage. "This would never have happened on Jupiter," she fumed. "Nor on any of the other planets. Even those scruffy Martians don't go on like this."

Katy's mum started rattling cups in the kitchen. "I suppose we'll have to call the police," she grumbled, pouring cocoa for everyone. "Tramping about on my clean floors, making a mess." But she seemed thankful that the break-in hadn't been worse, and she opened a packet of chocolate biscuits, although Katy's dad was only allowed one because of his diet.

"Well, it could have been a lot worse," he said, picking chocolate crumbs carefully from his shirt and licking them off his finger. "Apart from Katy's bike, nothing of any great value seems to be missing." He reached for the phone and was dialling the local police station when a sound from the doorway made them all turn round. Jane was standing there scowling like a coming thunderstorm.

"Nothing of any value?" she said, her voice almost squeaking with rage. "What about my spaceship? We left it in the garage, didn't we? Well, it's N O T T H E R E N O W!"

There was silence for a moment while everybody stared at everybody else. The family had completely forgotten their visitor's small two-seater spacecraft, which she'd hidden in the garage before they left for Boggy Bay.

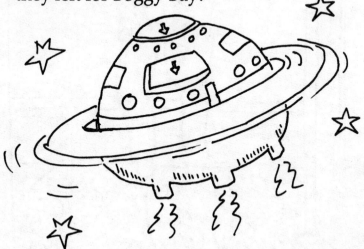

Katy groaned and laid her head on the kitchen table. The one thing she had looked forward to during the whole of Jane's visit was the time when she would take off back to Jupiter and leave them all in peace. Now she could be here for ever, and it didn't bear thinking about.

Mr Stuart opened and closed his mouth a couple of times and then stammered into the phone.

"I...er...er...sorry. Wrong number," he blurted out, dropping the receiver.

"I can hardly report a stolen spaceship, can I?" he said lamely, looking round at the others. "I'd feel a proper fool."

Mrs Stuart slapped her husband's hand as he reached absent-mindedly for another biscuit. "How's the poor girl supposed to get home now? Flap her arms and fly all the way?" she said.

"You'll have to report it, Dad," said Katy anxiously. "You can't have kids zooming around the sky in spaceships. They'll damage something."

Jane plodded gloomily to the table and sat down. "Don't talk stupid," she said, glowering at Katy as if it were all her fault. "Nobody could possibly be zooming around the sky. Not in my spaceship, anyway. The solar battery's flat, remember, through lack of sunshine in this awful weather you call summer. And it couldn't have re-charged while it was in the garage out of the sun all last week."

14

She held out a flat black object the size of a calculator. "In any case the ship won't take off without this. It's the computer that operates all the controls, and I never leave it on board. It was locked in my box upstairs."

"So whoever stole the spaceship must have just wheeled it away." Katy's mum frowned. "It's not very big, is it? They probably thought it was some sort of toy."

Mr Stuart looked brighter at once. "In that case it can't be all that far away," he said cheerfully. "It's probably around the town somewhere, in some kid's back garden. You can all start looking for it tomorrow while I'm at work."

"Not me," said Katy, swallowing the last of her cocoa and staring glumly down in to the mud at the bottom of the cup. "Term starts tomorrow. I've got to go back to school."

Jane gaped at her, her green eyes round as soup plates. "School?" she said excitedly, her scowls disappearing like magic. She beamed in delight. "I'll come with you, Katy," she declared. "The spaceship can wait. Making a report on Earth schools is much more important."

"It'll be very interesting for you," said Mr Stuart, nodding his head in approval, and sneaking off with a handful of biscuits when his wife wasn't looking.

Katy's mum took the cups to the sink. "It'll keep you out of mischief for a bit," she said shortly. "For a few days, anyway. Until the spaceship turns up."

Katy thought of Jane's enormous orange webbed feet and her rude, bossy manners. She thought of that strange habit she had of sending objects flying around the room using only the force of her own will-power. She thought of Mrs Mould, the worst teacher in the school, with her baggy grey stockings and a face to match. She thought of a meeting between the two, and her heart turned over like a dead goldfish.

"You must be joking!" she said loudly, pushing her chair back and glaring at them. "If you think I'm taking HER to school with me, you've got another think coming!"

Katy fled upstairs to her room and flung herself face-down on the bed. She wouldn't take Jane to school, she vowed. Not if she was the last person in the universe.

Chapter Two

The square, sagging face of Mrs Mould loomed over Katy. "What did you say the girl's name was?" she demanded, her eyebrows disappearing under her stiff permed fringe of hair. "And where is she from? This is most irregular, you know."

Katy quaked in her shoes and was unable to speak. The worst had happened, and here she was at school with Jane after all. Tantrums and hunger-strikes had had no effect. Even her dad had been on Jane's

side this time. Katy, deserted by her only ally, had found herself with no choice but to give in.

Jane scowled up at the teacher defiantly. "You know perfectly well what my name is," she said, astonishing Katy with her Australian accent. "I'm Jane Brown. Mr Stuart telephoned your headmaster this morning to ask permission for me to come. Surely he told you that I'm Katy's cousin from Australia, here on an educational visit."

Katy heard Polly Plum snigger in the back row. There were other snorts and giggles as Mrs Mould stared at the newcomer as if she couldn't believe her ears. Then the teacher's eyes narrowed and she placed her hands on her hips.

"And do all children in Australia wear gumboots in the classroom?" she enquired icily.

A ripple of laughter ran round the room and Katy's mouth went dry. This was the moment she had been dreading. If Mrs

Mould made Jane take off her boots the fox would really be among the canaries, for Jupitan feet were like nothing on Earth. Adapted for life on a watery planet, they were large, orange and webbed. The whole class would have hysterics, especially that idiot Polly Plum.

"Please, Mrs Mould," Katy burst out. "Jane can't take her boots off. She's got a sort of disease." Ignoring Jane's outraged gasp, Katy babbled hurriedly on. "It's her toes, you see ... they're covered with a sort of fungus that grows in Australian swamps ... a bit like warts ... only a hundred times worse..." Katy's voice tailed off and she glanced quickly at Jane, who had stopped scowling and was staring at her admiringly.

Mrs Mould moved her large bulk in its

24

tent-shaped purple dress hastily behind her desk.

"We certainly don't want anybody else catching that sort of thing," she shuddered. "Keep the boots on, for heaven's sake. And you'd better both sit down. Near the front, please, where I can keep an eye on you."

Katy breathed again as she sank into a seat in the front row. And as the lessons began and the morning passed peacefully on, she began to hope that her worries had been for nothing.

Even break time in the playground
went well, with the whole class gathering
curiously round the visitor to ask questions about the Australian swamps and to
find out whether she kept a koala bear for
a pet. Jane, who knew nothing at all about
Australia, talked so much rubbish that
Katy almost giggled aloud. And although
there were plenty of nudges and stares,
not one single person mentioned the
boots, much to Katy's relief.

It was the Science lesson that started the trouble. When the class filed back into the classroom after break, they found that Mr Graham had taken Mrs Mould's place and was busy drawing a small circle in the middle of the blackboard.

Katy settled in her desk and smiled happily. Mr Graham was her favourite teacher, and Science was her favourite lesson.

Mr Graham smiled back. Then he pointed towards the circle on the blackboard. "Today I want to talk about the planets in the Solar System," he said. "And the reasons why only Earth is able to support life. Imagine this circle to be the sun. Now, can anyone come out and draw for me the positions of the other planets?"

There was a clatter near the back of the room as Freddy Wilson, the class expert, swaggered forward and took the chalk. And it was obvious that he knew his stuff, for a plan of the Solar System swiftly took shape, showing Mars, Mercury, Venus and all the others, including Saturn with its famous rings.

Katy kept glancing anxiously sideways at the next desk. Jane was having such trouble keeping her face straight that she had to hide her head in her desk and stuff her hanky in her mouth to stop herself from laughing out loud. Finally, when

Freddy was in the middle of describing Jupiter itself, it all became too much for her. She gave such a loud snort of laughter that the whole class turned to stare, and Katy groaned in despair.

"Is something the matter?" asked Mr Graham pleasantly. "Does our young Australian visitor disagree? You're quite welcome to come out and show us your version, even if it is probably upside down."

Everybody giggled at Mr Graham's joke. Everybody, that is, except Jane. She stood up, plodded out to the front of the class and snatched the chalk from Freddy Wilson's hand. She thoroughly cleaned the blackboard, and then began to sketch a solar system such as nobody had ever seen before.

She drew the planets all roughly the same size, and all about the same distance from the sun. She explained that they rotated in exactly the same way as Earth, and were equally capable of supporting life.

"In fact, human beings colonised all the

planets thousands of years ago," she finished triumphantly, dusting the chalk from her fingers. "And millions of people live and work there, just like they do here."

There was an astonished silence when she had finished. Then Freddy Wilson gave a great guffaw that caused a snigger all round the room. Jane scowled ferociously and stamped her boots in temper.

Mr Graham was beaming all over his face. "That's quite enough, everybody," he said. "Jane's theory is a very clever one." He turned to Jane with a grin. "But what our young friend hasn't explained is why all our scientific discoveries tell us a completely different story. Space probes have actually landed on some of these planets, Jane, and found no life at all."

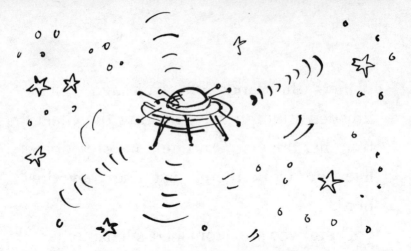

Jane shrugged. "It's all rubbish," she said. "Every space mission from Earth is deliberately fed all sorts of wrong information by the Inter-planetary Relations Board satellites. And all the real planets have special shields round them, to make them invisible, and to keep you lot from landing on them."

Mr Graham was still smiling and shaking his head. "But why should anyone want to do that?" he asked. "Surely they would want to be friends with Earth people?"

"Oh, they do," said Jane wearily. "But can you imagine what would happen? Earth would want to take over the whole galaxy, and there'd be nuclear war in no time. So the Inter-planetary Relations Board works night and day to keep it all a secret . . ."

Jane's voice suddenly faltered. She blushed crimson and then turned pale, putting her hand over her mouth and walking stiffly back to her place. Katy couldn't help feeling sorry for her, even though it had been Jane's own stupid showing-off which had got her into this mess.

"I made it all up," said Jane hurriedly as she sat down. "None of it's true, of course. It was just a joke." And she hid her face among some papers on her desk.

Mr Graham stared at her for a moment, his mouth gaping open. "Well, it was some joke," he said admiringly. "You almost had me convinced for a moment. And I bet this stupid lot believed every word!" Still chuckling, he turned and cleaned Jane's drawing off the board.

The class grinned sheepishly at one another. Katy let out a long sigh of relief as the bell rang for lunch. School with Jupiter Jane was providing some hair-raising moments, and the afternoon lessons were still to come.

Chapter Three

The first lesson of the afternoon was Maths. Mrs Mould gave out a bundle of typed sheets of paper, and everybody groaned aloud when they saw a long list of problems of the sort that begin, "If it takes seventeen men five and three-quarter hours to paint eight hundred and eleven metres of fence ..."

"These should keep you busy for a while," said Mrs Mould. "I want no talking, mind. And nobody helping anybody else. This is a test." She stared hard at Katy as she said it, as if Katy were the biggest cheat in the school.

For a while Katy's face grew hotter and hotter and her brain stubbornly refused to work. Then a folded piece of paper landed on her desk and she snatched it up. Opening the note in her lap, Katy read the answers to all fifteen questions, and raised her eyes to see Jane grinning at her from the next desk.

"Simple!" whispered Jane, waving something small and black in Katy's direction. "Easy as apple pie with this." Katy stared at the flat black object in Jane's hand, and her heart sank into her school dinner.

The floorboards creaked and a shadow fell across Katy's desk. A hand came from nowhere and the computer was snatched from Jane's grasp.

"And what is T H I S?" thundered Mrs Mould, who could move very quietly in spite of her bulk. "Using a C A L C U L A T O R? In a M A T H S lesson?" She held up the object for the rest of the class to see.

Everyone sucked in their breath and went "Ooh" and "Aah" as they nudged one another in delighted horror. Polly Plum had to be thumped on the back as she choked on another fit of giggles, and some of the boys even drummed their feet on the floor, until a look from Mrs Mould froze them to their seats.

Katy saw Jane's eyes flash with that familiar golden light and knew that a row was coming. She wished she could crawl into a crack in the floorboards and not come out again until Christmas.

Jane stood up and her face turned

the colour of beetroot soup. "It's not a calculator, it's a C O M P U T E R," she said loudly and distinctly, as if speaking to a half-witted chimpanzee. "We always use them for Maths where I come from. What's the point of spending hours and hours doing something that only takes half a minute?"

Jane turned to glare fiercely at the rest of the class. "It's stupid, like everything else on your stupid planet. I'll have to make a report about this." Sitting down abruptly again, she took a blue notebook from her pocket and began to scribble.

There was a long silence. Mrs Mould's breath rasped in and out like Katy's Auntie Brenda's who has asthma. Her nostrils flared like those of an angry dragon, and Katy watched fearfully, half-expecting to see smoke coming out. The whole class cowered, waiting for the storm.

"I think the headmaster had better hear about this," hissed Mrs Mould at last through clenched teeth. "The rest of you may get on with your Maths. These two young ladies had better come with me."

The school corridors were empty at that time of day as everybody was in class. Katy and Jane had to hurry to keep up with

Mrs Mould as she stomped grimly down
the stairs and across the main school hall
towards the headmaster's study.

"Er, I wouldn't fiddle with that if I were
you, Mrs Mould," said Jane suddenly, and
Katy saw that the teacher was irritably
tapping the keys of the computer as they
went along. "It's a very sensitive instru-
ment, you see, and if you touch the
wrong button you could...OH LORD, YOU
SHOULDN'T HAVE DONE THAT!"

41

Katy heard a sort of muffled shriek as Mrs Mould suddenly disappeared. Then she rubbed her eyes and stared upwards, unable to believe what she saw.

Mrs Mould, her eyes bulging in astonishment, was floating face down near the hall ceiling like an immense purple balloon.

"Help! G . . . get me down!" she croaked, her voice wobbly with fright.

"Stupid old bat!" muttered Jane. "I told you not to touch it. Get yourself down, if you're that clever."

Katy grabbed Jane's shoulders and shook her hard. "Get her down this minute!" she shouted. "You can't leave her up there all topsy-turvy. What if somebody comes in and sees her? We'll get into terrible trouble." She gazed up, fixing her eyes on the huge purple shape. "And if she falls she could really hurt herself."

43

Jane folded her arms. "It's her own fault," she said crossly. "I told her not to touch the computer. She must have pressed the anti-gravity button. She's dead lucky that ceiling's in the way, or she could be halfway to the moon by now. Anyway, I can only get her down if she gives me the blooming thing back."

Mrs Mould, still clutching the computer, began to buzz round and round the ceiling like a giant bluebottle trapped in a jamjar.

She jabbed frantically at button after button, but the only effect was to make her go faster or slower, or turn somersaults in the air. Finally she managed to grab the corner of the tall art cupboard near the wall. Gasping and panting, she heaved herself into a sitting position on the top.

Flinging the computer down at Jane's head, Mrs Mould began to shout at the top of her voice, and it was while she was perched there, shrieking, that the headmaster came out of his room.

There was total silence for a moment.

Jane stared at Katy and Katy stared at Jane. The headmaster stared at Mrs Mould, sitting red-faced on top of the art cupboard. Mrs Mould stared at the floor.

This wasn't half going to take some explaining, Katy told herself with a long, weary sigh.

Chapter Four

Katy and her classmates ran out through the school gates and down the hill towards the common, with Jane following as fast as she could in her clumsy boots.

"What happened to Old Mouldy, then?" Freddy Wilson asked Katy. "Why have we been let out of school so early?"

"Mrs Mould wasn't feeling well," Katy told him, blushing with shame. "Mr Lockett had to take her home."

"She's gone batty," giggled Polly Plum,

scampering past with her curls flying. "They say she climbed up on top of the art cupboard like a monkey and wouldn't come down. Coo, what a laugh!"

They all raced off, sniggering and talking, and Katy stood for a moment to watch them go.

"You could have cost the poor woman her job," she muttered sourly, as Jane caught up with her.

"Knickers!" retorted Jane. "She'll get over it soon enough, and everybody will forget all about it. Anything was better than telling Mr Lockett the truth."

Katy had reluctantly agreed to pretend that they knew nothing at all about what had really happened. They had let Mrs Mould do all the explaining, and of course the headmaster hadn't believed a single

word of the hysterical teacher's garbled
story. He had awkwardly helped her
down from the cupboard by means of the
window-cleaner's ladder, and had driven
her home for a few days' rest, putting the
whole incident down to overwork and
stress.

Katy felt guilty and uncomfortable, as
well as being sorry for Mrs Mould, so she
hardly spoke to Jane as they made their
way down towards the town.

49

"What's going on down there?" said
Jane suddenly, pointing down the hill.
"Look, Katy. They're making some sort of
playground on the common."

Faint music reached Katy's ears and her
heart beat faster as she stared at the scene
in front of them.

"It's a fair!" she cried, her face lighting up. "You know, roundabouts and coconut shies and cotton candy and helter-skelters and stuff. I'd forgotten it was coming this week."

Jane's face glowed with delight. "A real fair?" she cried, almost dancing off the

the ground in her excitement. "With gipsy caravans and fortune tellers and dodgem-car rides? I've read about them, but I've never seen a real one. We don't have them on Jupiter. Come on, Katy. I have to see this!" And Jane set off down the hill as fast as her boots would let her, almost tumbling over in her haste.

Katy raced after her and together they walked round the field. It was a busy and exciting scene, with men shouting at one another and hammering and banging as they erected tents and awnings, swings and slides. There were trailers and caravans parked under the trees.

Jane stared about her, a look of disgust on her face. "I don't think much of this," she said.

But before Katy could answer, a gruff voice from behind called out, "Get outa the way." The girls were suddenly pushed rudely aside as a red-haired boy on a bicycle wobbled past over the ruts in the grass.

"What cheek!" said Jane angrily. "I'll soon fix him." And she swiftly raised the fingers of her right hand and pointed them at the boy's retreating back.

"Wait!" said Katy, who was staring after the boy. "Look, Jane, that's my bicycle. I recognise the woollen cover on the seat. It's a bit off my dad's old jumper."

Jane grabbed Katy's hand, hopping gleefully from one foot to the other. "Let's follow him, Katy," she urged. "You know what this means, don't you? If he pinched your bike, the chances are he pinched my spaceship as well. He could lead us straight to it." And she hurried off after the boy.

When Katy found her again a few moments later Jane was standing transfixed in front of a children's merry-go-round, and the bicycle lay on the ground nearby. The red-headed boy was talking to a dark-eyed man with a wrinkled sunburnt face. The man was lying on his back bolting a small wooden car to the revolving platform of the roundabout. There were little wooden steam engines, tractors, buses, speedboats and other models, and there was one object in particular that made Katy gasp out loud.

It was a small silver spacecraft, with an open hatch and two small seats inside. There was a control desk, several metal levers, and an outer covering which had square black panels set all along the sides. These were just like the solar heating panels Katy had seen on the roof of that posh new house down the street.

"I wouldn't bolt that down if I were you," said Jane boldly to the man as he wriggled over to the ship with his spanner. "It belongs to me."

The man stuck an astonished face out from underneath.

"Gerrout of that!" he shouted. "Watcha mean, it belongs to you? I bought it only yesterday off the scrap dealer, this lad's father. I paid ... 'Ere, watcha think you're doing?" He suddenly got up and scrambled off the platform as if it were on fire as a faint rumbling began to shake the metal frame.

Jane had reached out and slipped her portable computer into a slot in the control panel in the ship. Katy's heart almost stopped beating as the spaceship suddenly lit up all over with a faint green glow. The fairground man stepped back, gaping in astonishment, his face as pale as plaster.

The boy with red hair made a sort of moaning noise and disappeared rapidly into the distance.

Jane climbed quickly into the ship through the front hatch and turned to Katy, grinning.

"Come on, Katy," she said, pulling a silver helmet over her pigtails. "Want a lift home?"

Faced with the thought of an irate fairground man to cope with if she stayed behind, Katy didn't really have much choice. She scrambled hastily into the passenger seat of the spaceship.

"I thought you said the batteries were flat," she said, her voice coming out faint and squeaky. Jane grinned at her over her shoulder.

"There's been quite a bit of sunshine in the last couple of days," she said confidently. "We'll have managed to store a bit of power. Not enough to get me away from Earth's atmosphere, of course. But probably enough to reach your back garden." She pulled a few levers and green and red lights began to flash on the control panel. "Keep your fingers crossed, Katy. Here we go!"

Katy caught a brief glimpse of the fairground man flinging himself face down on the grass with his arms over his head as the spaceship shuddered gently and then silently lifted into the air. Dogs barked and leaped wildly aside and people began to run from all corners of the field, shouting and waving their arms.

Katy grinned and waved back cheerfully, with a feeling that her visitor wasn't so bad after all. Everything had turned out right in the end, and Katy couldn't help giggling when she realised that the detested bicycle had now probably disappeared for ever. But best of all, the spaceship had been found, and it wouldn't be long before Jane was on her way back to Jupiter where she belonged.

Singing cheerfully at the controls, Jane

expertly guided the ship away from the fairground, over the tall buildings of the town and then they skimmed down over the rooftops towards Katy's house.

"Isn't this great, Katy!" she called excitedly. "Isn't this just the greatest thing that ever was!"

Katy didn't reply. She was much too busy throwing up over the side, and wishing she had never heard of a girl called Jupiter Jane.

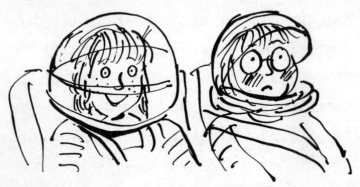